Emily and Alice
Baby-Sit Burton

Written by
Joyce Champion

Illustrated by
Joan Parazette

Gulliver Books • Harcourt, Inc.
San Diego   New York   London

www.harcourt.com

Gulliver Books is a trademark of Harcourt, Inc., registered in
the United States of America and/or other jurisdictions.

Library of Congress Cataloging-in-Publication Data
Champion, Joyce.
Emily and Alice baby-sit Burton/Joyce Champion;
illustrated by Joan Parazette.
p. cm.
"Gulliver Books."
Summary: When Emily and Alice accept their first baby-sitting job,
they must learn how to care for their unusual charge, a bulldog jealous
of the new human baby in its household.
[1. Babysitters—Fiction. 2. Dogs—Fiction.]
I. Parazette, Joan, ill. II. Title.
PZ7.C3585Ep 2001
[E]—dc21   99-6187
ISBN 0-15-202184-1

First edition
A C E G H F D B

Printed in Singapore

The illustrations in this book were done in
pen-and-ink and watercolor on Arches hot-press paper.
The display type was set in Remedy Double and Caxton Bold.
The text type was set in Perpetua.
Printed and bound by Tien Wah Press, Singapore
This book was printed on totally chlorine-free Nymolla Matte Art paper.
Production supervision by Sandra Grebenar and Pascha Gerlinger
Designed by Lori McThomas Buley

In loving memory of Michael
and for Mom
—J. C.

For Max, Isabel, and Holden,
and for Suzi, who can baby-sit
—J. P.

Best Baby-Sitters

Emily and her best friend, Alice, were tired of Chuckie Jones. All Chuckie talked about was his new baby brother.

"My little brother kicks when I wiggle his toes," Chuckie bragged during school. "You should hear the cute sounds he makes when I do this." Chuckie made silly faces.

"*And,*" Chuckie bragged, "my baby brother smiles only for me. No one else."

"I *know* we can get that baby to smile for us," Emily told Chuckie.

Emily went to Alice's house after school. "We have to become baby-sitters, Alice," she said. "We can baby-sit for Chuckie's little brother. And, we will make him smile."

"What if the baby doesn't want to smile for us?" asked Alice. "What if he only wants to cry?"

"Don't worry," said Emily. "We've had lots of practice."

"We have?" asked Alice.

"Yes," said Emily. "We practiced on our dolls. We practiced on my little sister, Nora. We'll be the best baby-sitters ever."

Emily and Alice made business cards.

The next day, Emily and Alice ran to Chuckie Jones's house. Burton, Chuckie's bulldog, was in the yard. Burton was usually a friendly dog. But Burton didn't run over to meet Emily and Alice. He didn't get up, or even open his eyes.

"I wonder what's wrong with Burton?" asked Alice.
"I don't know," said Emily. "Maybe he just wants to sleep."

Emily and Alice knocked on the door. Mrs. Jones came out, holding a baby bottle. Emily looked at Alice and smiled. She gave Mrs. Jones one of their baby-sitting cards.

Mrs. Jones looked at the card and thought for a moment.

"Yes," she said. "I think I can use some baby-sitters."

Emily squeezed Alice's hand.

Mrs. Jones invited the girls inside. They looked at Chuckie's baby brother. He was asleep in his cradle.

"See?" Emily whispered to Alice. "Baby-sitting will be easy."

"When can you start?" Mrs. Jones asked.

"We can take the baby right now," said Emily.

Mrs. Jones smiled. "Oh no," she said. "I don't need baby-sitters for the baby. I need baby-sitters for *Burton*. Burton has not been a happy dog."

"Baby-sit *Burton*?" Emily and Alice asked.

Mrs. Jones nodded.

Emily and Alice sighed…and agreed to baby-sit a bulldog.

Baby-Sitting Burton

Alice pulled on Burton's leash. Emily pushed Burton's hind legs. But Burton would not get up. Mrs. Jones was right. Burton was not a happy dog.

Burton sighed and lowered his head to his paws. It was the saddest sigh ever to come from a dog.

"Get up, Burton," Emily said. "Let's play!"

Emily found a Frisbee in Burton's doghouse. She threw it. "Go get it, boy!" she shouted.

Burton did not move.

"This is not good," said Alice. She sat down and patted Burton's head.

"I know what will work," said Emily. She whispered into Alice's ear, "Food. A dog will do anything for food."

"Burton, come to my house," said Emily. "I will give you a peanut butter cookie."

Burton opened one eye.

"I will give you a peanut butter cookie, too," said Alice.

Burton opened his other eye. He stood up slowly
and walked to Emily's house with his head down.

Alice held out a peanut butter cookie. Burton sniffed it and sighed. He didn't want a cookie. He crawled under Emily's bed and wouldn't come out.

"This is *really* not good," said Alice. "What kind of baby-sitters are we?"

"We are the *best* baby-sitters," said Emily. "And we can't give up."

Emily and Alice crawled under the bed with lots of cookies.

"Yummy, yum," Emily said to Burton. "Sweet peanut butter cookies."

Burton turned and faced the wall.

"Don't be such a *baby*," said Emily.

Burton looked at Emily. His eyes opened wide. He put his head back and howled.

"Baby?" Emily said again.

Burton groaned, long and loud.

"I think that Burton doesn't like the word *baby*," said Alice.

Burton moaned and sighed.

"I think," said Emily, "that Burton doesn't like *Mrs. Jones's* baby."

Burton covered his face with his paws.

"Emily," whispered Alice, "what can we do with a dog who doesn't like a new baby?"

Emily and Alice tried to think, while Burton whimpered in the corner.

Burton the Baby

Alice patted Burton's head. "You are a good little dog," she said.

Burton licked Alice's hand.

Emily smiled. "Burton is a good little *puppy*," she said.

Burton slowly wagged his tail.

"Is little Burton cold?" asked Emily. She found a
doll's blanket to cover him.

Burton rested his head in Emily's hands.
"Awwww," said Alice. "What a cute little boy."

Alice tied a baby bonnet around Burton's face.

"You are our sweet baby puppy," Emily and Alice told Burton.

Burton crawled out from under the bed. He was a silly-looking bulldog, but he looked happy.

It was hard for Emily and Alice not to laugh. But they wanted to be good baby-sitters. And good baby-sitters would never laugh at a dog that needed to be a puppy.

Emily and Alice picked up Burton. They put him
into Emily's doll stroller. Then Alice gave him a baby
bottle. Emily gave him some toys. Burton snuggled
under the covers.

Alice helped Emily push Burton outside.

The Tupper twins were down the street, playing basketball. They stopped and looked into the stroller.

"What a cute little puppy," Robin Tupper said in a very high voice.

Randy Tupper grinned at Burton. "Hey, Chuckie," he called, "come here!"

Chuckie Jones looked at his dog.

"Burton?" he said. "What have Emily and Alice done to you?"

Burton chewed on a toy.

"Burton needs to be a puppy now," Emily told Chuckie.

Burton thumped his tail.

Alice made funny faces at Burton. Burton made silly sounds back.

"You made Burton happy," said Chuckie. "Too bad dogs can't smile like baby brothers do." He laughed and walked down the block.

Emily and Alice turned the corner. They tucked Burton in. They smiled at him—and Burton's lips curled up.

It was as close to a smile as a bulldog could get. It was a smile that was meant for Emily and Alice—and no one else.